KT-176-891

PUFFIN BOOKS

Published by the Penguin Group: London, New York, Australia,
Canada, India, Ireland, New Zealand and South Africa
Penguin Books Ltd, Registered Offices:
80 Strand, London WC2R 0RL, England

puffinbooks.com

First published by Hamish Hamilton 1984
Published in Picture Puffins 1995
This edition published in 2007
10 9 8 7 6 5 4 3 2 1

Text copyright © Holt, Rinehart and Winston 1967
Copyright renewed 1995 by Bill Martin Jr
Copyright © the Estate of Bill Martin Jr, 2004
Illustrations copyright © Eric Carle, 1992
All rights reserved

The moral right of the author and
illustrator has been asserted

Made and printed in China

ISBN: 978–0–141–50159–8

Brown Bear, Brown Bear, What Do You See?

By Bill Martin Jr

Pictures by Eric Carle

PUFFIN

Brown Bear,
Brown Bear,
What do you see?

I see a red bird
looking at me.

Red Bird,
Red Bird,
What do you see?

I see a yellow duck
looking at me.

Yellow Duck,
Yellow Duck,
What do you see?

I see a blue horse
looking at me.

Blue Horse,
Blue Horse,
What do you see?

I see a green frog
looking at me.

Green Frog,
Green Frog,
What do you see?

I see a purple cat
looking at me.

Purple Cat,
Purple Cat,
What do you see?

I see a white dog
looking at me.

White Dog,
White Dog,
What do you see?

I see a black sheep
looking at me.

Black Sheep,
Black Sheep,
What do you see?

I see a goldfish
looking at me.

Goldfish,
Goldfish,
What do you see?

I see a teacher
looking at me.

Teacher,
Teacher,
What do you see?

I see children
looking at me.

Children,
Children,
What do you see?

We see a brown bear,   a red bird,

a green frog,

a black sheep,   a goldfish,

a yellow duck,

a blue horse,

a purple cat,

a white dog,

and a teacher
looking at us.
That's what we see.

Some other books by Eric Carle

Polar Bear, Polar Bear, What Do You Hear?

This playful story combines animals, colours and sounds in a rowdy menagerie that children will enjoy imitating.

Panda Bear, Panda Bear, What Do You See?

Gently rhythmic text is accompanied by iconic images from Eric Carle in this special book about endangered species.

Baby Bear, Baby Bear, What Do You See?

A celebration of wildlife and the special bond between mother and child. The final title in the series.

The Bad-Tempered Ladybird

The bad-tempered ladybird thinks she's bigger and better than everyone else and picks fights with every animal she meets, but she soon learns the importance of friends.

The Very Hungry Caterpillar

A small and very hungry caterpillar nibbles his way through the pages of this classic book with die-cut pages and finger-sized holes to explore.

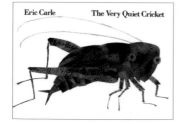

The Very Quiet Cricket

The story of a little cricket and his song. Sound chip included.

The Very Busy Spider

A little spider spins all day long until her new web is finished. A book to *feel* as well as read.